PRINCESS POSEY

and the

MONSTER STEW

Stephanie Greene

ILLUSTRATED BY

Stephanie Roth Sisson

G. P. PUTNAM'S SONS
AN IMPRINT OF PENGUIN GROUP (USA) INC.

Also available

1

PRINCESS POSEY and the **FIRST GRADE PARADE**

2

PRINCESS POSEY and the **PERFECT PRESENT**

3

PRINCESS POSEY and the **NEXT-DOOR DOG**

For Deb Gonzales.—S.G.

*For the Youngs: George, Dina,
George and Bella—S.R.S.*

G. P. PUTNAM'S SONS

A division of Penguin Young Readers Group. Published by The Penguin Group.
Penguin Group (USA) Inc., 375 Hudson Street, New York, NY 10014, U.S.A.
Penguin Group (Canada), 90 Eglinton Avenue East, Suite 700, Toronto,
Ontario M4P 2Y3, Canada (a division of Pearson Penguin Canada Inc.).
Penguin Books Ltd, 80 Strand, London WC2R 0RL, England.
Penguin Ireland, 25 St. Stephen's Green, Dublin 2, Ireland
(a division of Penguin Books Ltd.).
Penguin Group (Australia), 250 Camberwell Road, Camberwell, Victoria 3124,
Australia (a division of Pearson Australia Group Pty Ltd).
Penguin Books India Pvt Ltd, 11 Community Centre, Panchsheel Park,
New Delhi—110 017, India.
Penguin Group (NZ), 67 Apollo Drive, Rosedale, Auckland 0632, New Zealand
(a division of Pearson New Zealand Ltd).
Penguin Books (South Africa) (Pty) Ltd, 24 Sturdee Avenue,
Rosebank, Johannesburg 2196, South Africa.
Penguin Books Ltd, Registered Offices: 80 Strand, London WC2R 0RL, England.

Published simultaneously in Canada.
Printed in the United States of America.
Decorative graphics by Marikka Tamura. Design by Marikka Tamura.
Text set in Stempel Garamond.
Library of Congress Cataloging-in-Publication Data
Greene, Stephanie.
Princess Posey and the monster stew / Stephanie Greene ; illustrated by Stephanie
Roth Sisson. p. cm.— (Princess Posey ; 4)
Summary: First-grader Posey and her friends are excited about Halloween, but also a
little nervous about trick-or-treating and eating Miss Lee's monster stew.
[1. Halloween—Fiction. 2. Teachers—Fiction. 3. Schools—Fiction. 4. Friendship—
Fiction.] I. Sisson, Stephanie Roth, ill. II. Title.   PZ7.G8434Pp 2012
[E]—dc23   2011020632
ISBN 978-0-399-25464-2
1 3 5 7 9 10 8 6 4 2

5/13

CONTENTS

FLASHLIGHTS ARE FOR BABIES

ou children are like wiggly

rms this week," Miss Lee said.

Posey laughed.

Everyone else in the class did, too.

Halloween was only two days

away. It was so hard to sit still!

Yesterday, they drew pictures of pumpkins and witches. They played a counting game with black cats.

Today, they were writing Halloween stories.

Miss Lee let them work with th friends because it was special.

"You can talk quietly," Miss said. "I will come around and how everyone is doing."

Posey and Ava and Nikki were working together.

So were Luca and Nate. They sat at the next table.

Posey was writing a story about a ghost. It wanted to carry a flashlight when it went trick-or-treating.

"The ghost is afraid of the dark," she told Nikki and Ava.

"That's so funny," said Ava.

"I carried a flashlight last year," Nikki said.

"Me too," said Ava.

Posey had, too.

In kindergarten, she was afraid of the dark. Gramps had given Posey his flashlight to carry.

It was as bright as the sun. It lit up the dark street and made Posey feel safe.

Trick-or-treating was exciting. But it was a little scary, too.

"Are you going to carry one this year?" asked Nikki.

Posey was about to say "maybe" when Luca interrupted.

"Flashlights are for babies," he said.

THE FUNNEST TIME
OF THE YEAR

"**L**uca, you be quiet," said Posey.

Boys were so annoying! Posey wished Luca and Nate sat farther away.

"Only babies are afraid of the dark," Luca said.

"Yeah. Girls are scaredy-cats," said Nate.

"They are not!" said Posey.

"Boys are scaredy-cats!" Ava said.

Miss Lee came over to them. "It doesn't sound as if you're talking about your stories," she said.

"Luca is listening to us," Posey said.

"They're talking so loud," said Luca.

"I think you all need to get back to work," said Miss Lee.

She waited while they started to write again.

When the phone on her desk rang, Miss Lee went to answer it.

Posey turned her back so Luca couldn't hear.

"I have excitement bubbles in my stomach," she whispered. She bounced once on her bottom. "Pop!"

"I have excitement bubbles, too," Ava said. "Pop!"

Nikki said "Pop!" too.

Soon everyone near them was saying "Pop!" and bouncing on their chairs.

Miss Lee hung up the phone. "Boys and girls," she said.

The popping stopped.

"That was Mrs. Warski." Miss Lee smiled. "Her class is going to join us for our Halloween party. We will make monster stew."

Monster stew!

That sounded so scary.

Everyone wanted to know what
monster stew was, but Miss Lee
just laughed. "You will have to wait
until Friday to find out," she said.

"What if there's a real monster in it?" Posey said.

"What if the monster's still alive?" said Ava.

"It will scream when we eat it," Nikki said.

The girls shrieked. They grabbed one another's hands. It was so much fun to be scared together.

Halloween was the funnest time of the year.

A REAL BEAUTY

Gramps picked Posey up after school. Her mom was at the doctor's office with Danny. It was his one-year checkup.

Posey and Gramps stopped to buy two pumpkins: a big one for Posey, a baby one for Danny.

"I picked a real beauty, didn't I, Gramps?" Posey said proudly when they got back in his truck.

"You sure did," he said.

Posey's pumpkin was almost perfectly round. It only had one flat spot.

Gramps said that was where it lay on the ground while it grew. When he saw it, he had called it a "real beauty."

That meant he liked it.

When they got home, Posey tried to lift the pumpkin out of the back of the truck. It was too heavy.

"Here, let me do that,"
said Gramps.

He carried her pumpkin into the kitchen. He cut off the top.

Posey's job was to scoop out the seeds. It was hard work.

"Do you need some help with that?" asked Gramps.

Posey held her spoon tighter. The seeds were slippery.

"The seeds on the bottom are stuck," she said.

"You may have to get your hands dirty," said Gramps. He pushed up the sleeves of Posey's shirt. "Now you can dig in," he said.

Posey reached her hands into the pumpkin. She pulled out a clump of seeds. They had long strings dangling from them.

Gramps held out a bowl for her to put them in.

"Remember last year when Nick and Tyler tricked me?" Posey said.

Nick and Tyler lived next door. They loved to tease her.

Last
Halloween,
they told Posey
to close her eyes
and reach inside their pumpkin.

Posey's fingers felt something cold and slippery.

"It's witch's brains," Nick said in a spooky voice.

Posey had a bad dream after that.

"You were pretty scared, as I remember," said Gramps.

"That's because I was five," Posey said. "They can't scare me this year. I'm six."

"I guess that means you don't need my flashlight for trick-or-treating," said Gramps.

"No way!" said Posey. "Flash-lights are for babies."

Posey plunged her hands into the pumpkin again.

She wasn't going to be afraid of anything this year.

She wasn't.

POOR DANNY

When Posey's mom came home with Danny, he had streaks of tears on his face.

"Uh-oh," Gramps said. "Looks like someone didn't like his check-up."

"He screamed when he got his shot," said Posey's mom.

"I don't blame him," said Posey.

"Then we stopped at Hank's Store on the way home," Posey's mom said. "The ghost Hank puts near the front door every year scared him."

Posey knew that ghost. It looked like a white sheet with two huge black eyes.

The first time Posey walked past it, the ghost shook and made spooky noises.

She had been scared of it, too.

"Poor little guy. Come to Gramps." He held Danny in his lap.

"Don't worry, Danny," Posey said. She squeezed his cheeks. "Ghosts aren't real. They are only make-believe."

"How did you two do with the pumpkins?" Posey's mom asked.

"Great," said Posey.

"I'm waiting for Posey to draw the face she wants me to carve," Gramps said.

"I'll go get my marker." Posey got up from the couch.

"Bring down your costume for Gramps to see," said her mom.

"Okay!" Posey ran up to her room. Her costume was hanging in her closet.

Her mom had made a beautiful dress with sparkly material. When Posey moved, the whole dress sparkled.

She put it on and ran back downstairs.

"That was quick," Gramps said. "What happened to your tutu?"

"It's right here." Posey lifted up her dress.

Her mom and Gramps laughed.

"Are you going to wear them both?" her mom said.

"Of course," said Posey.

She always wore her tutu. She put it on every day after school.

Posey never told anyone, but when she wore her tutu, she was Princess Posey.

Princess Posey could go any-where and do anything.

All by herself.

"Come over here for a minute," said Gramps.

Posey stood in front of him.

"I want to see if that glow is coming from your dress or from inside you," Gramps said. He held

Posey's
ear and
pretended
to peer
inside.

Posey giggled
and squirmed. It tickled!

"Just what I thought." Gramps
let go of her ear. "You are glowing
from the inside out."

Posey twirled to make her dress
billow out.

"Did you ask Gramps if he will
help you make your hat?" her mom
asked.

"Will you, Gramps?" said Posey.

"Sure," said Gramps. "I guess you need a fireman's hat with that costume."

"Noooo . . ." Posey knew he was teasing.

"Do you need a baseball hat?"

"Gramps! I need a princess hat!" Posey said.

"Oh-h-h, a princess hat," Gramps said. "Why didn't you say so? I'll come over tomorrow afternoon."

THE OGRE'S EYEBALL

The next afternoon, Posey sat on the steps to wait for Gramps.

She could hardly wait to show him her drawing of the hat. She had made it up herself.

"Hey, Posey!" a voice called. "Come see our costumes."

Tyler was in his driveway. He had a silver helmet on his head.

Posey ran next door.

Tyler's arms and legs were silver, too. He had huge gloves on his hands.

"I know what you're supposed to be," said Posey. "An astronaut."

"Right," Tyler said. "I wrapped tinfoil around my football helmet and everything. These are my hockey gloves."

"You look so real," said Posey. "What is Nick going to be?"

"A really gross ogre," said Tyler. "Here he comes."

The back door of his house slammed.

The ogre that came out didn't look like Nick at all.

It had straggly gray hair and a hunched back. It was dressed in ripped clothes. It walked with a limp.

The scariest part was the ogre's face.

One of his eyeballs drooped. His nose looked broken. His face was full of wrinkles.

The closer the ogre got, the more real it looked.

Posey stepped back.

"What are you scared of?" Tyler said. "It's a rubber mask."

"I don't like those," said Posey.

She had touched a rubber mask in the store one time. It felt cold. Like dead skin.

"Say something to her, Nick," said Tyler.

"Trick or treat," Nick said in a growly voice. "Catch."

He threw something to her.

Posey caught it. Yuck! It was sticky and slimy.

Posey looked down.

It was the ogre's eyeball.

"YOU'RE A SCAREDY-CAT!"

Posey screamed. She dropped the eyeball and rubbed her hands against her pants.

Nick and Tyler laughed.

"Hey, be careful with that," said Nick. He took off his mask. The gray hair came off with it.

It was Nick, all right.

He picked up the eyeball and stuck it on his mask. "How do you expect me to see without my eyeball?" he said.

"You're so mean, Nick!" Posey shouted. She stomped back to her own yard.

"What's wrong, scaredy-cat?" Tyler shouted. "I thought you were a big kid now!"

"I'm not a scaredy-cat," Posey shouted. "You're a scaredy-cat!"

Gramps had pulled into the driveway.

"Sounds like those two are up to their old tricks," he said. "What did they do this time?"

Posey told him about the sticky eyeball.

"I guess you have to expect that kind of gag on Halloween," Gramps said. "From the sound of it, you took care of yourself."

He held open the door. "Come on. Let's go make that hat."

Gramps whistled when he saw Posey's drawing.

"Pretty fancy stuff," he said.

"Where did you get this idea?"

"From my imagination," said Posey.

Her drawing showed a tall, pointed hat. It looked like a wizard's hat, except it was pink.

"I want to cut stars all over it," she said. "And those little moons that look like a C."

"That's a crescent moon," Gramps said.

"I like those," Posey said. "I'm going to put glitter on it so it sparkles. I want ribbons to come out of the top."

Princess Hat

"It's quite a hat," Gramps said. "I'm proud of you."

"There won't be another one like it, will there?" Posey said.

"Not unless there's another Posey," said Gramps.

Posey and Gramps got to work.

Making her hat was so much fun. Posey almost forgot about the ogre's eyeball.

But not quite.

CHAPTER
SEVEN

JUST LIKE
A FLASHLIGHT

Posey told her mom about the eyeball while she got ready for bed.

"It wasn't real," Posey said.

"But you thought it was at first," said her mom.

"It felt real," said
Posey. She squeezed
toothpaste onto
her brush.

"Are you okay about it now?" her mom asked.

"Yes. But Danny wouldn't like it."

"No." Her mom smiled. "About all Danny can take at his age is his bumblebee costume."

"He should carry Gramps's flashlight so he won't be scared," said Posey.

"Good idea," said her mom. "That reminds me. Mrs. Romero brought over something for you today. I'll be right back."

Posey brushed her teeth and turned on her night-light.

Then she got into bed.

Her mom came back and sat on the edge.

"Mrs. Romero thought you could wear this tomorrow night," she said.

She gave Posey a paper bag. There was a large plastic circle inside.

It was pale pink.

"Mrs. Romero said it's called a glow necklace," her mom said.

"When you bend it a bit, it will glow pink."

It was pretty. Posey thought it would be fun to wear a glowing pink necklace.

"It will be just like having a flashlight," her mom said. "Except you don't have to hold it."

Just like a flashlight? Posey frowned.

She put the necklace on her bedside table.

"Don't you like it?" her mom said.

"Flashlights are for babies," said Posey.

"Oh. I see." Her mom looked at her for a minute. "It was nice of Mrs. Romero to give it to you," she said.

"I know," said Posey.

"You need to thank her tomorrow."

"I will."

Her mom stood up.

"Mom?" Posey said. "What do you think will be in the monster stew?"

"Are you still worried about that?" said her mom.

"What do you think will?"

"Oh . . . I don't know." Her mom smiled. "All kinds of silly, funny things. It's make-believe, remember?"

"I remember."

After her mom went downstairs, Posey got out of bed.

She went to her drawer and took out her tutu. She brought it into bed and put it under the covers.

Posey knew monster stew was make-believe. But sometimes make-believe felt as real as real.

Like the eyeball.

Posey held her tutu against her face. Princess Posey was brave. She wouldn't be afraid of monster stew or going trick-or-treating without a flashlight.

Posey wouldn't be afraid, either.

CHAPTER
EIGHT

MONSTER STEW

When Posey got to school the next day, it looked like Halloween.

She walked past the principal on her way to Miss Lee's class. The principal had a red ball on her nose. She wore a green wig.

"I know what you are," Posey said. "You're a clown."

The teachers were wearing costumes, too. Some wore witch's hats. One teacher had a pretend wart on the tip of his nose.

Miss Lee wore black pants and a black shirt. The shirt had a cat made out of orange sequins on the front.

Posey was so excited. Everyone was. It was hard to do normal work.

Miss Lee let them go outside for a long recess. When they got back to the room, there was a table in front of her desk.

It was covered with an orange tablecloth.

In the middle of the table was a large black pot.

Smoke was coming out of it. Everyone got quiet when they saw it.

"It's a witch's pot," Posey whispered.

"It's for the monster stew," said Nikki.

"What do you think is in there?" Ava asked. She sounded scared.

"Make-believe stuff," Posey said.

"Like what?" said Ava.

The boys had crowded in front of the table. They pushed and shoved. They tried to look in.

"Careful, boys," said Miss Lee.

"We want to know what's in it," said Luca.

"All sorts of scary things that you're going to love, Luca," Miss Lee teased. "Like bat's blood and lizard's livers."

"Cool," Luca said.

"What about eyeballs?" said Will. "My brother said his had eyeballs."

"That's right, Will. Monster eyeballs." Miss Lee laughed. "Now, go and sit down, all of you."

Monster eyeballs! Posey rubbed her hands against her pants.

She was not going to eat that stew.

"What if we don't want to eat it?" Ava whispered.

"They can't make us," Posey said.

"But what if they do?"

Poor Ava! She sounded as if she was going to cry.

Posey had to do something.

"I'm going to tell Miss Lee," she said.

KEEPING
A SECRET

Posey marched up to Miss Lee's desk. Miss Lee was putting things in a large box.

"Miss Lee, no one can make us eat that stew," Posey declared.

"Make you? What an idea, Posey!" Miss Lee said. "No one has to eat it if they don't want to."

"Ava's afraid," Posey said.

"Ava doesn't have to be afraid. I promise." Miss Lee leaned down. "Can you keep a secret?" she whispered.

Posey nodded. Keeping a secret was important.

Especially if it was for Miss Lee.

"These are the lizard's livers." Miss Lee lifted a plastic bag out of the box just high enough for Posey to see. It was filled with raisins.

Posey's eyes got big.

"And these"—Miss Lee held up another bag—"are the monster's eyeballs."

Grapes!

The monster's eyeballs were green grapes! They were peeled so they looked slimy.

Posey clapped her hands over her mouth.

"You can tell Ava she doesn't need to worry," Miss Lee said. "But don't ruin it for anyone else, okay?"

"Okay," said Posey.

She hurried back to Ava and Nikki.

"Don't be afraid," she told Ava. "It's so funny. I promise."

Miss Lee's and Mrs. Warski's classes loved the monster stew. They laughed and shouted every time Miss Lee put in another silly thing.

"And now, for the final ingredient," Miss Lee said at the end. She held up a pitcher. "Bat's blood!"

"That's grape juice!" they all shouted.

Posey and Ava and Nikki had so much fun.

It was the best Halloween ever.

GLOWING FROM
THE INSIDE OUT

"Let me go first, Mom," Posey said.

"Okay," said her mom.

Posey ran ahead up Mrs. Romero's front walk.

A pumpkin with a crooked

smile sat beside the door. A candle flickered inside.

Night was all around. Other children were trick-or-treating up and down the street.

Posey knocked on Mrs. Romero's door.

She heard Hero bark inside. Then footsteps.

"Trick or treat!" Posey shouted when Mrs. Romero opened her door.

"Why, Posey!" Mrs. Romero said. "You are the most sparkly princess I have ever seen."

"Gramps said I look like a moonbeam," said Posey.

"He's right," said Mrs. Romero.

"Where's Hero?" said Posey. "I wanted him to see."

"I put him in the study," said Mrs. Romero. "Some children are afraid of dogs."

Posey's mom came onto the porch with Danny.

"What do you have inside your hat?" Mrs. Romero asked. "The stars and moons are shining."

"It's your necklace," said Posey. "I didn't need it outside. I needed it inside."

"That's about the prettiest thing I've ever seen," Mrs. Romero said. She held out a bowl of candy. "Take one for yourself and one for Danny, too."

Posey took a piece of candy for herself. She put another one in Danny's pumpkin.

"Did you thank Mrs. Romero?" her mom said.

"Thank you!" Posey sang.

She skipped back down the walk and onto the sidewalk.

A group of boys was walking past. One of them was an ogre.

"Trick or treat," he said in a growly voice.

"You don't scare me, Nick," Posey said.

"Cool hat," said the ogre.

It was so much fun to be out at night. The dark was so exciting.

Posey floated from house to house. She glowed from the inside out the whole way.

P⚘SEY'S PAGES

It was so much fun to make my princess hat!
You can make your own, too. You need a
pencil, a large piece of poster board, scissors,
tape and/or glue sticks, glitter glue, ribbons,
a stapler, a piece of elastic, and a glow stick.

1. Draw a semicircle from one corner
of the poster board to the
other. Make a mark in the
center of the straight edge.

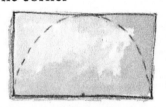

2. Cut out the semicircle. It will be
curled into a cone with the center
mark as the point of your hat.

3. Trace stars and moons in the middle of
the poster board and cut them out.

4. Decorate the hat with glitter glue—as much
as you want. Let it dry.

5. If you want ribbons to come out of the tip, glue them inside.

6. Curl your semicircle into a cone, making the bottom fit the top of your head.

7. Staple the overlapping ends along the bottom and then tape and glue them together from top to bottom. Let the glue dry.

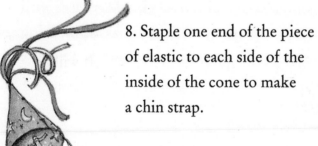

8. Staple one end of the piece of elastic to each side of the inside of the cone to make a chin strap.

9. Twist the glow stick to make it glow. Tape it inside the hat.

10. Put your hat on and secure the elastic under your chin. Happy Halloween!!!!

Watch for the next **PRINCESS POSEY** book!

PRINCESS POSEY
and the
TINY TREASURE

Posey knows the rules about bringing a treasure to school. It has to stay in your backpack or cubby or else Miss Lee will take it away. But Posey has something very special to show Ava and Nikki. It's so small—surely it's okay if it stays in her pocket?